Magic Farm

A Big Surprise!

Ashley Birch

EGMONT

This book belongs to:

....

With special thanks to Valerie Wilding
For Zac, Rory and Esme

EGMONT

We bring stories to life

Magic Farm: A Big Surprise!
First published in Great Britain 2011
by Egmont UK Limited
239 Kensington High Street
London W8 6SA

ISBN 978 1 4052 5527 1

1 3 5 7 9 10 8 6 4 2

www.egmont.co.uk

A CIP catalogue record for this title is available from the British Library

Printed and bound in Great Britain by CPI

CONTENTS

Strawberry Surprise

Woof! Woof!

'Shush, Max!' Olly gently ruffled the glossy black and white fur of the Thompson family's new sheepdog. With his spare hand, he hugged a little white lamb. 'And don't you start bleating, Woolly!'

Baaa!

'Olly, try to keep them quiet,' whispered Olly's friend, Aidan.

They crept along the outside of the farmhouse wall, keeping low until they were beneath the kitchen window sill. Olly bobbed up for a quick peek. His sister, Hannah, was at the kitchen sink, washing a huge basketful of strawberries.

Olly grinned as Aidan fixed a large metal hook to the end of an old fishing rod.

Baaa!

'Quiet, Woolly!' Aidan whispered. He edged up and peeped through the open window, then ducked down again. 'Hannah's filling a bowl with some of the strawberries. Wait till she takes them to the fridge and leaves the basket.'

Olly heard Hannah's flip-flops slapping across the kitchen floor. 'Now!' he said, leaping up.

Aidan jumped up too, and poked

the fishing rod through the window. He quickly hooked the basket of strawberries and swung it out into Olly's waiting arms.

The boys laughed softly as they heard Hannah gasp.

'Who's there?' she said.

Woolly poked her little nose into the strawberries and began nibbling.

Olly pulled the basket away and Woolly's nose came out stained pink. She bobbed her head happily; strawberries tasted good!

'Stop it, Woolly,' Olly whispered.

The lamb bleated and the tiny bell round her neck tinkled.

'*Now* I know who it is!' came Hannah's voice.

Her face appeared at the window.
'You two are so terrible!' she said.
'Don't let Woolly have any more –
she'll finish the lot. They're the nicest
strawberries ever!'

'And we grew them on our very
own farm,' Olly added proudly. 'Hey!
Where's Max?'

'He's here,' said Hannah. 'He ran

in to see me.' She brought him out, leading him with a finger hooked under his collar.

Max was a working dog – he wasn't meant to be in the farmhouse. The Thompsons hadn't lived on Golden Valley Farm very long and they were getting new animals all the time. They already had a horse and some chickens, and now that they had sheep they needed a dog to help look after them. They'd bought Max from a nearby farmer, and Dad had built him a brand new kennel. Max had a comfy bed in there, and his own cosy blue blanket. He loved his new home in the farmyard!

Max started barking excitedly and

Woolly darted away, springing across the grass.

'Come back here, Woolly!' Olly shouted, running after her.

Max chased them both. An escaped lamb? This was his job!

Aidan grabbed a big handful of strawberries. 'Here, Woolly! Here, Woolly, Woolly, Woolly!'

The lamb raced back to Aidan and leapt at him, squashing the handful of strawberries. Over they both went! Olly and Hannah burst out laughing as their friend lay in the grass with Woolly nibbling at his strawberry-stained face.

'Get off me!' Aidan spluttered.

Olly picked up the lamb, cuddling

her close. Woolly felt warm and soft
in his arms.

'Don't get attached to her, Olly,'
said Aidan, smiling. 'Lambs aren't

pets – they're farm animals, like Max. Shouldn't Woolly be with your other sheep?'

'I think she should,' said Hannah. 'She's already flooded the bathroom floor.'

Olly giggled. 'Yeah, she jumped in the bath with me!' He hugged Woolly tight. 'Aah, she's no trouble.

She follows me everywhere.'

'Sometimes that's a nuisance though, even if she is cute,' said Hannah. 'Remember when Woolly joined in our football game and headbutted the ball into the river?'

'Exactly,' said Aidan. 'So why don't we go somewhere we know Woolly can't follow us?'

'Like where?' asked Hannah.

Aidan grinned. 'Like Magic Farm?'

Off to Magic Farm!

'Great idea! I'm game,' said Hannah.

'What about you, Olly?'

'You bet!'

Olly took the lamb to the sheep pen. 'Sorry, Woolly,' he said, 'but you

can't come with me this time.' Then

he told Max, 'On guard!' The dog sat

on his haunches outside the pen.

Olly watched him for a moment to

make sure he stayed, then went back

over to Hannah and Aidan. As they headed for the top of the hill behind Golden Valley Farm, Olly could still hear the lamb bleating, but he tried hard not to look round.

Hannah laughed. 'Woolly's calling you, Olly.'

Aidan bleated, 'O-o-o-Olly!' Olly grabbed a pine cone and threatened to throw it at him. Aidan ducked and ran ahead. 'You can't get *meeeee*!' he called back.

The three friends darted through the trees then headed down the other side of the hill towards a large scarecrow that stood stiffly, one arm outstretched. But Hannah, Olly and Aidan knew that it was no ordinary scarecrow. It held a magic secret!

Aidan's long legs got him there first. He skidded to a stop, grabbed the scarecrow's outstretched arm, and span it round. The scarecrow turned with him, and suddenly Aidan vanished!

Hannah was next. Olly watched as she whirled round and disappeared.

He knew exactly where they'd gone. Magic Farm!

'My turn.' Olly grabbed the arm and span round with the scarecrow. All the colours of the grass and sky, trees and flowers whooshed into a silvery whirlwind. Olly found himself stumbling into Hannah and Aidan. He'd made it!

Olly flopped happily on to the grass, which was so bright it almost seemed to shimmer. He looked up at the puffball clouds floating above them. Some were palest pink, some soft blue and others a lovely gold.

'Aren't they just gorgeous?' said Hannah.

Olly gazed at the sun. It glittered

like an enormous diamond, shooting out sparks of rainbow colours. 'It's nothing like our sun, is it?' he said. 'You can stare at it without hurting your eyes.' He turned to look further down the slope at the pretty honey-coloured farmhouse, with scarlet creeper climbing over it. Last time they had been here it had looked so peaceful, nestled amid the fields and garden and orchard. But today it looked like something strange was going on.

What's happening on Magic Farm? Olly wondered. *The Hayseeds seem to be in trouble . . .*

Three scarecrows were running around wildly, waving about their straw-stuffed arms. They were the Hayseeds, a family of friendly scarecrows who had woken up one morning to find themselves on Magic Farm. The farmhouse had been empty and . . . well, someone had to look after all the animals and raise the crops. But sometimes they didn't get things quite right. This looked like one of those times.

'Come on,' said Olly. 'Let's see if we can help.'

'Bet they're having problems with the Little Rotters again,' said Hannah, scrambling to her feet.

The Little Rotters were naughty, greedy creatures, the size of gnomes. Their cheeky, grinning faces, topped

by tufty, bright orange hair, were always popping up where there was trouble.

'I wonder what's gone wrong now?' said Hannah as she followed Olly and climbed the white picket fence around the farmyard. Aidan was so tall that he leapt straight over it.

'Hey, Sunny!' Olly called over to a

scarecrow in a big yellow hat. 'What's up?'

'Hellooo!' Another, very scruffy scarecrow called Muck noticed them first, and waved. 'Look, everyone, it's the children!'

'Ha-ha-hat-*tish*oo!' sneezed a third scarecrow. He snatched at his hat as it flew off, but it sailed towards Aidan.

Aidan caught it and gave it back. 'Here you go, Tishoo!'

Sunny's usually cheerful face looked worried. 'It's the –' she began, but her voice was drowned out by a chugging, clanking, jangling noise.

Out of a red-painted barn trundled a big purple machine.

Slowly, the machine moved closer.

It wasn't a combine harvester, or a tractor or a steam engine. It looked like a mixture of all three, and it was driven by another of the children's scarecrow friends, Patch. Olly knew what the strange machine was.

'The Duzzit!' he cried. If you asked the Hayseeds how they got the grass cut so quickly, or how they mended the barn roof in no time at all, they'd always say, 'The Duzzit does it!'

When Patch saw they had visitors he pulled a shiny golden chain and the Duzzit's steam whistle went off. *Wheeeeup! Wheeeeup!* He switched off the engine and the bell on the front of the machine jangled one last time. Then there was silence.

Now that all the noise had stopped, Sunny was finally able to answer Olly's question. 'We're having trouble with the sheep,' she said.

'They won't graze,' added Muck. 'Someone has scattered sawdust all over the field so our sheep can't feed themselves! We think it was the Little Rotters.' Now that he looked closely, Olly could see fine yellow sawdust sprinkled amongst the shimmering blades of grass.

'We've got to move the sheep and

their pen into another field, quickly. Otherwise they'll all starve!' Patch called from the Duzzit's driving seat.

He started the machine up again. It huffed, puffed, clanged and jangled as it moved off.

'Why is Patch in such a tizzy?' Olly asked Sunny. 'What's the rush?'

Sunny looked serious. 'It's not just

that the sheep will go hungry. If they aren't safely back in their pen in a new field before the sun goes down, the lambs will be in danger.'

Muck gulped, and mouthed a single word. 'Foxes!'

Runaway Snowball

Sunny, Tishoo and Muck all hurried after the Duzzit.

'They'll never round up the sheep with the Duzzit making that much noise,' said Olly.

'I wonder how we can help?' Hannah said.

'They need a sheepdog,' said Aidan. 'Like your Max. There must be one somewhere. All farms with sheep have a sheepdog. I'll take a look.' He raced away.

Hannah and Olly were just about to run after Aidan, when the whitest, fluffiest, *sparkliest* sheep they'd ever seen ran past, chased by Muck.

'You stop, Snowball!' the scarecrow shouted.

Baaaa!

'Wow,' said Hannah, smiling. 'That sheep really does look like a giant snowball.'

'On legs!' said Olly with a grin.

'Come on, let's help catch him.'

They split up. Every time Snowball got away from Muck, either Olly or Hannah jumped out, flapping their arms, trying to stop him escaping. Whenever poor Muck dived for the sheep, Snowball leapt into the air with a *Baaa!*

'Snowball's got legs like Aidan,'

Olly panted. 'Super-springy!'

Snowball bleated happily and sprang into a wheelbarrow and out again, then headed for the pig sty. Round and round he went. *Baaa! Baaa! Baaa!*

'Come back here, you naughty sheep,' Muck wailed, tripping over his own feet.

'I'll go round the pig sty one way,'
Hannah said to Olly, 'you go the
other way, and we'll trap him in
the middle.'

But Snowball was too fast. All they
could do was touch his glittering
snow-white coat before he bounded
away again. Muck shook his head in
despair, scattering pieces of straw.

'Look at him go,' Hannah panted.
'They should have called him Bouncy
Ball, not Snowball. Oh!'

Olly skidded to a sudden stop.

'What's happened now?'

Hannah pointed. 'There, by the gate to the sheep pen. Little Rotters!'

Olly looked. Little grinning faces. Orange tufts of hair. Hannah was right. They were Little Rotters!

'So that's the cause of the bother,' he said. 'Muck was right – it *was* the Little Rotters who put the sawdust

in the field. Never mind them now, though, Hannah. We can deal with them later. First, we need to help Muck. Where's Snowball got to?'

'There!' cried Hannah. 'Oh dear.'

Yet again, Snowball was heading straight for the sty where the pigs lived. Muck was chasing after the sheep, his arms spread wide.

Snowball sprang on to an upturned bucket, and leapt straight over the wall into the sty.

Olly ran over to look. Snowball was rolling in gloopy mud, watched by two startled pink and black pigs with super-curly tails. 'Oh no!' Olly said. 'Snowball's a mudball now! He's definitely not sparkly any more!'

'Uh-oh!' said Hannah, as Muck leant over to try to reach the sheep. 'Quick, Olly! Grab Muck's legs before he falls in!'

But before they could move Muck toppled over the wall, head down in the mud, and feet kicking in the air.

'Too late!' said Olly. He took hold of the scarecrow's legs. 'Don't you

worry, Muck. We'll get you out.'

'Muck's name suits him more than

ever today,' giggled Hannah, as Olly

heaved and tugged, trying to pull the scarecrow out. Suddenly, with a great *thlurp*! he was free.

Muck stood, swaying slightly. His head was plastered with thick brown mud. A strip of potato peel hung over one eye, and gloop dripped from the end of his nose. 'I'm fine,' he said in a wobbly voice. 'But please don't let

Snowball get away again.'

But the naughty sheep jumped straight back out of the pig sty and disappeared towards the vegetable garden.

'Ha-ha-hat-TISHOO-OO-oo-oo! Ha-ha-ha-hat-TISHOO-OO-oo-oo-oo!'

Olly was startled. 'Was that Tishoo?' he asked Hannah.

'Who else!' she replied. 'He's in the vegetable garden. Maybe he's finally caught Snowball. Let's go and see.'

Poor Tishoo hadn't caught him. He hadn't caught *any* sheep. There were loads of them, all different colours and patterns, darting between rows of vegetables and jumping over bushes, bleating wildly. 'I can't catch any of them,' Tishoo wailed.

'Don't worry, Tishoo, we'll help you,' said Hannah.

'It won't be easy though,' said Olly, looking round at all the chaos. 'Those sheep think they're playing hide and seek.'

Tishoo, Olly and Hannah dodged in between sweetcorn and cucumber plants, trying to catch the tricky sheep. They knocked their shins on giant watermelons and squished fallen tomatoes – but didn't catch a single sheep.

Finally, Olly flopped down on to a huge pink pumpkin for a breather. 'Phew!'

'Olly!' Hannah shouted. 'Snowball's

heading straight for you. Grab him!'

Olly sprang up quickly, but muddy Snowball skidded on some squashed tomatoes, bumped into a melon, tumbled into Olly and sent him flying backwards over the pumpkin.

Laughing, Hannah pulled him to his feet. 'You were meant to catch

Snowball, Olly. Not the other way around!'

'Hey!' Olly pointed. 'There's Aidan. Look what's behind him!'

The Sheep-goose

Aidan saw all the mayhem in the vegetable garden and grinned. 'You lot look like you need help.'

'Dead right!' said Olly. 'I thought you went to find us a sheepdog. Look

out! There's a stroppy-looking goose

behind you.'

Aidan glanced round. 'I know. She

looks fierce, doesn't she?'

'She does,' said Hannah. 'But where

is the sheepdog?'

'I've looked all over Magic Farm and I can't find one,' said Aidan. 'But I saw the goose rounding up some chickens, then she tried to herd some cows and I thought, *Why not?*'

'Why not what?' said Olly.

'Why not turn a goose into – a sheep-goose! Say hello to Shoo.'

Olly just stared, but Hannah bent

down and said, 'Hello, Shoo.'

HOARRK!

Hannah fell back in surprise. Shoo waggled her tail and waddled off towards the sheep.

'Let's see if she can manage on her own,' said Aidan.

Shoo didn't have much success. She *hoarrked* and *hoarrked*, but the sheep just ignored her, doing exactly as they pleased.

'I don't know what we're going to do,' Tishoo said. He glanced anxiously around, checking for foxes.

'I wonder if I can help Shoo,' said Aidan. 'I'm not bad with sheepdogs.' He put finger and thumb between his lips and gave a high-pitched whistle.

'Back home, that whistle tells the dog to go behind the sheep.' He did it again, louder.

Shoo looked round. *Hoarrk*! She immediately waddled round behind a sheep who'd found some tasty carrot tops to nibble.

'Brilliant! The goose understands you,' said Olly.

'I know!' crowed Aidan. 'I speak goose!'

After more whistles, and a lot of bossy *hoarrk*ing from Shoo, a few of the sheep, including Snowball, had arranged themselves in a small group.

Sunny, Patch and Muck heard the whistles and came to watch.

'You're a good whistler, Aidan,' said Sunny. 'I'm going to try!' She copied him, putting a finger and thumb to her mouth. She blew. Nothing happened.

'It's your stitching. It's letting air out,' Hannah said. 'Patch can whistle with grass. We saw him last time we were here. Why don't you get him to show you how to do it?'

'Can you teach me too, Patch?' Olly asked the scarecrow. 'I can't whistle like Aidan.'

The scarecrow showed them how to clasp their hands with a blade of grass between their thumbs. 'Now put it to your mouth and blow,' he told them. 'Like this!' He made a screeching whistle sound.

Eeeeeee!

Sunny and Olly had a go, and were soon making the screechy noise too.

'Now copy my whistle-tune,' said Aidan. 'One at a time, otherwise Shoo will end up even more confused than the sheep.'

Aidan showed them three more whistles: one for 'Go right!', one for 'Go left!' and another for 'Look out – sheep escaping!' Then he, Olly and Sunny arranged themselves around the vegetable patch. Taking turns, they each helped the bossy goose to steer the sheep towards the new field with its juicy-looking grass.

Eeeeeee! went Sunny on his blade of grass.

Eeee! instructed Olly.

Eeeeeee! Eeeeee! whistled Aidan.

Now the sheep trotted along obediently. *You'd never know they'd been so naughty*, thought Olly with a smile.

Hannah ran on to open the gate.

The scarecrows had just finished
putting together the pen in the new
field, and the fence posts were all
in place.

'They're almost all inside,' said Patch as the sheep trotted past.

Sunny glanced at the sky. 'Phew! In good time, too. The sun's just beginning to go down.'

'What a team!' said Olly. Suddenly, he heard a piercing whistle, and span round. 'Was that you, Aidan?'

'Nope, not me . . .'

Loud whistles now rang all around the farmyard. The Hayseeds stopped to listen. Shoo waddled the wrong way and a sheep broke away from the rest of the flock.

The whistles continued, and more of the sheep darted off towards the wrong field. Soon there were sheep roaming all over the place again.

'Olly . . . Aidan!' Hannah called. 'Someone's whistling to confuse the sheep! What shall we do?'

You Know Who

'Uh-oh,' said Olly. 'Bet I know who's whistling. Come on.' He ran round the back of the red barn, and started stamping his feet and waving his arms. 'You go away!' he shouted.

'Little Rotter! Go away!'

A small creature with orange hair and a wicked grin squealed and dashed behind the water trough.

Sunny shrieked in fright and all the Hayseeds huddled together, trembling.

'I can see you, Little Rotter!' cried Olly. 'We're not scarecrows. You don't frighten us!' He grabbed a broom and tried to sweep the naughty creature out of the farmyard.

Holding up its baggy trouser legs

so it didn't trip over them, the Little Rotter shot across the yard. Reaching the fence, it turned and made a nasty face. It didn't realise Olly had nearly caught up, and jumped in fright.

'Ug ug ug ug ug!' the Little Rotter yelped as it dodged the broom. It scrambled through the fence and ran towards the pond. Olly let it go, and stalked back to the barn.

'Great stuff, Olly!' said Hannah. 'But that wasn't the only Little Rotter whistling. There's at least one more up by the sheep's new field. Shoo's guarding the gate, so the Rotters can't scatter more sawdust.'

The Hayseeds were still in their tight huddle.

'We saw what you did,' said Muck. 'Thank you. You will be our friends forever!'

'You chased a Rotter away!' said Sunny. 'I'm so happy.'

'But I'm still worried,' Muck said. 'How can we stop the horrid things messing about with our sheep? There are foxes out there, remember.'

Olly looked around, thinking. 'We need to get the Rotters off the farm,' he said.

'Good idea, Olly,' Hannah agreed. 'Hayseeds, what do Little Rotters like more than anything? Even more than causing trouble?'

The scarecrows all spoke together. 'Playing in compost!'

'We put our grass cuttings and rotting fruit and leaves and dead flowers on the compost heap,' said Muck, 'and sometimes it smells just terrible! The Little Rotters play in it and they spread it everywhere.'

'Hmmm. I've got an idea. Can we have some of your compost?' Olly asked. He started to feel excited as a plan took shape in his head.

'Help yourselves,' said Patch. 'You'll find some buckets in the barn. We put them there for cleaning.'

Olly, Hannah and Aidan hurried to the red barn, then on to the compost heap, swinging two shiny buckets each.

As they neared the steaming pile

of compost, the awful smell suddenly hit them.

'Poo! Fancy playing in that,' said Hannah, as she shovelled rotting compost into a bucket. 'It smells *horrible*.'

Aidan tried to hold his nose and fill his buckets at the same time. It didn't work, so he let go of his nose

and shovelled as fast as he could. The face he pulled made Olly laugh out loud.

When the buckets were full, they carried them past the pond, behind the barn and round the sheep pen. The smell was so strong that Olly felt sure the Little Rotters would soon come to investigate.

'Are any Little Rotters following us?' he whispered.

'Yes,' hissed Aidan. 'Three. They think we can't see them.'

As Olly led the way out to the farm gate, he took a peek. Three orange tufts of hair were dodging from tree to tree. He could see the Little Rotters sniffing the air in delight.

'How can they like this smell?'
groaned Hannah. 'I feel queasy. Is it
much further?'

'We need to get at least halfway to the forest,' said Olly.

Hannah groaned again. 'We're not even at the gate yet.'

'Ooh, I feel ill,' moaned Aidan.

'OK,' said Hannah. 'Let's go for it. Hold your breath and . . . *ruuuun!*'

They sprinted along as fast as they could, with a bucket gripped in each hand. Six buckets clattered as the three friends ran.

Eventually, they made it past the gate, and soon they were nearly at the forest. Panting for breath, they all emptied their buckets.

'Poo!' cried Aidan.

'Fwoarr!' gasped Hannah.

When the last bucketful had

spludged on to the heap, they strolled away, glad to leave the smell behind them. All they could do now was wait.

Suddenly, they heard a squeal. Olly glanced round. 'Look!'

The Little Rotters were rolling over and over in the compost.

'Woo!' shrieked one.

'Weeeee!' shrieked another.

The third did a spectacular dive

right into the middle of the steaming

heap, shouting, 'Oooo! Lubbly lubbly lubbly!'

Hannah, Aidan and Olly gave each other a high-five.

'Very lubbly indeed!' said Olly.

Hoarrk! Hoarrk!

Back at the farmhouse, the Hayseeds handed the children glasses of milk and chocolate-chip cookies to celebrate. 'You sure you don't want a few chocolate chips?' Olly asked

Patch, who stood beside him.

'No,' the scarecrow said. 'They'd go straight through and come out of the hole in my jacket.'

'Never mind,' said Sunny, with a cheery smile. 'At least the Little Rotters are out of the way.'

'For a – ha-ha-hat-*tish*oo! – while, anyway,' said Tishoo. He dived

for his hat before it knocked
the heads off a clump of huge stripy
daffodils.

Shoo had led the last stray sheep into the new field, and Patch closed the gate behind them. Olly leant over the fence and gently stroked one of the sheep, who nudged a nose into his palm.

'I'll put the Duzzit away,' Patch said, 'now we've learnt how to work our sheep-goose! Plenty of other jobs on the farm for a clever Duzzit, and I'm sure we can keep Shoo busy too.' The goose gave a loud honk, as if in reply, and everyone laughed.

Patch climbed on the great purple machine, and started it up. *Grrrrrm! Rumble! Clang! Chugalugalugalug!*

Olly and the others clapped their hands over their ears.

'We have to go home now too, Patch!' shouted Olly. 'But we'll see you again soon.'

'I hope so . . .' they heard as Patch rode off with a chug and a clank and a jangle and a *wheeeup*!

They said goodbye to the other Hayseeds, and set off back to Golden Valley. As they walked, they heard a noise behind them.

Hoarrk!

'It's Shoo,' said Olly. 'Look, she's

following us back home.'

'She must like you,' giggled Aidan. 'Perhaps she wants to be your pet, like Woolly.'

Hoarrk! Hoarrk!

The children walked a little faster. So did the sheep-goose!

Hoarrk! Hoarrk! HOARRK!

Aidan laughed. 'She's herding us.'

'Look out!' Hannah squealed, as Shoo caught up with them. The goose herded them towards the scarecrow with the outstretched arm, her orange beak pecking at their ankles.

Aidan was first, as always. Round the scarecrow he went, and in a flash he was gone.

'Go on, Hannah, quick!' said Olly,

jumping away from the bossy Shoo.

When Hannah had disappeared, Olly grabbed the scarecrow's arm. 'Bye, Shoo! Clever sheep-goose!' he yelled. He ran round the scarecrow and, moments later, was back in Golden Valley.

Aidan was already halfway up the hill, heading for his home. 'See you again soon!' he shouted. 'Watch out for geese or escaping sheep.'

'Bye, Aidan!' Hannah and Olly hurried home, too.

As soon as they arrived, Woolly the lamb bounded over to Olly and nuzzled his hand.

'Sorry, little one,' said Olly. 'I've no food. Maybe I can find –'

But Woolly had danced away into the middle of a whole group of little lambs.

'Oh!' Olly looked disappointed. 'I thought she'd missed me, but she only wanted to see if I had anything to eat. It doesn't look as if she wants me any more.'

'I'm sure she still wants you to be

her friend,' said Hannah. 'It's just that it's fun for her doing lamby things with other lambs.'

Olly nodded. 'Yes, but –'

'Come on,' said Hannah. 'You know it's for the best. Woolly's not a pet, she's a farm animal – a Golden Valley Farm animal.'

'I suppose you're right,' he said.

'Sheep belong with other sheep, nice and safe in a field. And it's brilliant seeing Woolly so happy.'

'Right!' said Hannah. 'Let's go and see if Mum and Dad have left us any strawberries.'

They reached the farmhouse door and Olly looked back at their dog, Max, sitting in the sunshine, watching

over all the sheep.

'Max is doing such a good job,' he

said. 'I don't think we'll ever have to

get a sheep-goose for our farm!'

He followed his sister inside. It was lovely to be home at Golden Valley Farm, but he was looking forward to their next adventure too. You never could tell what might happen at good old Magic Farm!

EGMONT PRESS: ETHICAL PUBLISHING

Egmont Press is about turning writers into successful authors and children into passionate readers – producing books that enrich and entertain. As a responsible children's publisher, we go even further, considering the world in which our consumers are growing up.

Safety First
Naturally, all of our books meet legal safety requirements. But we go further than this; every book with play value is tested to the highest standards – if it fails, it's back to the drawing-board.

Made Fairly
We are working to ensure that the workers involved in our supply chain – the people that make our books – are treated with fairness and respect.

Responsible Forestry
We are committed to ensuring all our papers come from environmentally and socially responsible forest sources.

For more information, please visit our website at
www.egmont.co.uk/ethicalpublishing

There's lots more fun to be had at **Magic Farm!**

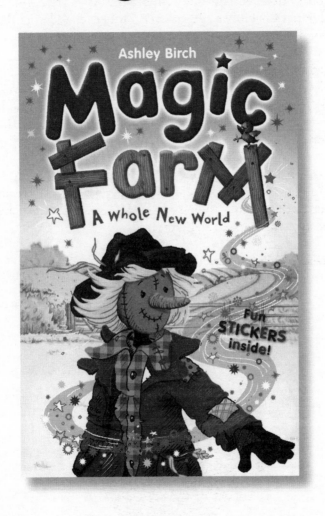